To read more about Stanley, look out for all the
Something Wickedly Weird books:

The Werewolf and the Ibis
The Ice Pirates
The Buccaneer's Bones
The Curse of the Wolf
The Smugglers' Secret
The Golden Labyrinth

Read more spooky tales in Dust 'n' Bones,
also by the award-winning Chris Mould.

And visit Chris at his website:
www.chrismouldink.com

THE ICE PIRATES

CHRIS MOULD

Hodder
Children's
Books

A division of Hachette Children's Books

For Sam and Abigail Mould

First published in Great Britain in 2007
by Hodder Children's Books
This paperback edition published 2010

1

A Catalogue record for this book is available from the British Library

ISBN 978 0 340 93103 5

Printed and bound in Great Britain by
CPI Bookmarque Ltd, Croydon, Surrey

The paper and board used in this paperback by Hodder Children's Books
are natural recyclable products made from wood grown in sustainable
forests. The manufacturing processes conform to the environmental
regulations of the country of origin.

Hodder Children's Books
A division of Hachette Children's Books
338 Euston Road, London NW1 3BH
An Hachette UK company
www.hachette.co.uk

Admiral Swift

A The Wooden Mile
B The Lighthouse
C The Old Pirate Wreck
D Candlestick Hall
E The Watchtowers
F The Church
G The Village Square
H The Sweet Tooth
I The Grinning Rat

Stanley Buggles stood on the station platform of the gloomy industrial town where he lived. He was fully prepared for his winter visit to Crampton Rock, swamped by two cases and a large bag, all filled with itchy woollen garments knitted by his grandmother.

A wave of anxiety ran over him. His first visit to the island had been filled with all manner of adventures and he wondered if his return would be as eventful. He was hoping for a more peaceful time, even if it was to be considerably colder.

His mother was there, with his stepfather at her side. She wore the most ridiculous fur coat that he hated because when she hugged him the hairs tickled his face.

Within minutes he was on the train, and as he sat waving goodbye to his weeping mother he made a gesture with his hand that indicated he would write.

The train creaked and groaned into a state of forward motion, finally hurtling onward into the darkness of an early winter's evening.

Stanley made himself comfortable and drifted into thoughts of the previous summer. It was six months since he'd inherited Candlestick Hall from his great-uncle, Admiral Bartholomew Swift. Stanley had never met him, but he knew every detail of his unfortunate death. A dark encounter with a fearsome werewolf had left him headless.

Now the winter came thick and fast, but Stanley had not slept peacefully since leaving Crampton Rock. Each night he dreamt of the Ibis, the great and ancient artefact that he had discovered hidden in the house.

It had rested quietly in the belly of the preserved pike that sat mounted on the wall. And in protecting its safety, Stanley had been forced to outwit the three deadly pirates that had darkened his door.

As the hardest season beat at the train window Stanley dreamed of the huge fire at Candlestick Hall and already he felt cosily warm.

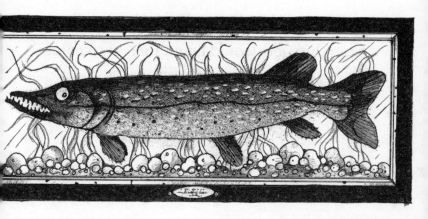

But the pike lay in his glass case, mumbling away to himself. He felt a warm hum from the precious gift that lay inside him, but he was not comfortable. Stanley had taken the Ibis out and held it in the warmth of his hands, and that could only lead to one thing. The chain of events that would put everything at risk had begun and nothing could put a stop to it. Of course he would try, but there was only so much he could do. He was confined to his see-through box on the wall.

The pike knew that, slowly but surely, the Stormbringers would begin their awakening. He had a daunting feeling that they were already on the move.

A gathering Storm

At the very moment that Stanley had held the precious Ibis in his hand, a crack had appeared in the ice, three thousand miles away. A month later, the first wisp of foggy breath had filtered out into the freezing cold air.

Something, somewhere, had been stirred and was very slowly coming back to life. Soon it would begin its long journey south, where it sensed the whereabouts of a lost prize.

An icy, skeletal hand
wriggled into life and forced
another crack in the cold
glassy tomb that held it fast.
Small movements rippled, then
suddenly its icy keep shattered
into a million pieces.

The bony prisoner was
freed. His body twitched.
Life and limb poured over
him in a grim display,
covering his frame. A
beastly beard grew
rapidly from his chin,
cascading down his
front, and a gallery of
tattoos began to draw
themselves over his
yellowed skin.

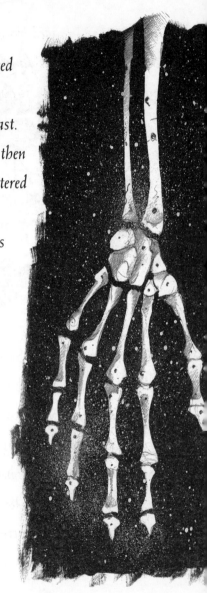

The torn and ragged clothes he had died in stitched themselves together, with a bullet belt over each shoulder and a shotgun strapped to his back.

And when he stood up, someone was there waiting, someone lean and lank and dreadful on the eye. The man's attire of grand velvet and lace was damp and foisty, and close up, spores of moss grew from its surface.

His hardened, bony face never acknowledged his bearded partner. Oh, but they were very much together. And, without speaking they set off into the night, armed to the teeth, through the gathering blizzard.

Stanley sat back in the train and closed his eyes. The summer, along with all its twists and turns, had been and gone. He thought of Mrs Carelli, the housekeeper of Candlestick Hall. She would be waiting for him, and right now he knew she would be baking fresh bread.

He could almost smell it. He had missed her cooking through the autumn. Perhaps there would be a bubbling stew to warm him when he arrived.

Within a short while the gentle rocking of the carriage had sent him plunging into sleep and he slumped peacefully against the window.

A great squeak and squeal grated through the air. The train was grinding to a halt. Stanley wiped a circle of condensation from the window and peered through the glass. By now the night was bleak and black. He could just make out the crooked wooden sign that bore the name of Crampton Rock. A voice came through the carriage:

'This train terminates at Crampton Rock. Please take all your belongings with you.'

Stanley stared around him in a dozed state. He was alone on the train. Nobody else would be getting off here, he thought.

Just as he'd hoped, Mrs Carelli was waiting for him.

19

She was so wrapped up against the bitter cold that he could only see her eyes and nose.

'You didn't have to come,' he said. 'I know the way now.'

'I wouldn't have missed it for the world,' she laughed, and threw a warm hug around him.

Stanley had prepared himself for the treacherous route to the island: the harsh drop of the steps from the cliff top and the rickety footway fashioned from old boat timbers that they called the Wooden Mile.

They made the slippery dangerous trek talking like old friends through their muffled mouths.

The planks of the Wooden Mile were

frosted and slippy and Stanley steadied himself nervously at every step. When the tide was in, there was no way to the island – the water would wash right over the top. But for now the way was clear.

The Wooden Mile passed through a cave on its way to the island and, as Stanley rounded the corner, he could finally see the village. Candlestick Hall looked fantastic in the silvery light from the frost.

Silhouettes of boat masts fronted the quayside, and the harbour lights lit the way. Lionel Grouse, the lighthouse keeper, was there to meet them. He called to them through the dark.

'Stanley, it is good to have you back. I would have come to the station but we have had trouble with a missing boat. All is fine now. Here, give me your things.'

Something Wickedly Weird

Stanley's long journey was over. As he
finally entered Candlestick Hall, he
could smell cooking.

His prayers had been answered! Something simmered on the stove top, inviting him to lift the lid.

In the front room a fire roared up the chimney, wood glowed, and sparks cracked and spat, holding Stanley in a hypnotic stare. He grabbed his favourite chair and threw himself into it. Everything was warm and peaceful.

'I'll sleep here tonight,' he announced. 'It's so cosy.'

'Whatever you wish, lad. It's fine by me. You're the master of the house and it's good to have you back, I must say. The old place has been quiet without you through the autumn,' said Mrs Carelli, her voice softening.

'Best batten down the hatches, though. Mister Grouse says there's a rare snowstorm coming this way from the north. A real beast of a blizzard blowing in with the wind, they reckon, like nothing we've ever seen before.'

The icy warriors marched on, never stopping or
speaking, simply heading south. Nothing could stand
in their way. They advanced over great mountains
and moved swiftly through caves and forests, all with
one aim: to make their destination and take what they
believed to be theirs.

3

The Stormbringers

Stanley woke in the night. He was downstairs alone. The roaring fire had eased itself into a gentle furnace, still lighting the space around the hearth. He could hear something, he was sure: a voice, whispering his name.

'Stanley. Stanley.'

It was coming from the hall, he thought. His heart beating faster, he left the warmth of the room for the darkness of the hallway, following the voice.

As he grew closer, he realized it was the pike in the glass case. Stanley had been so eager to come in from the cold and satisfy his hunger that he had neglected to pay the pike a visit.

He rubbed his tired eyes.

'Hello, Mister Pike,' he began. 'I am sorry I have not greeted you. I take it you still have hold of my friend the Ibis.'

Stanley received a sideways glance from the pike that suggested something was wrong. He was about to unscrew the case and check that the Ibis was still concealed inside, but the pike stopped him in his tracks.

'Do not hold her, Stanley,' he began.

'What?'

'You mean pardon. The word is pardon,' the pike insisted.

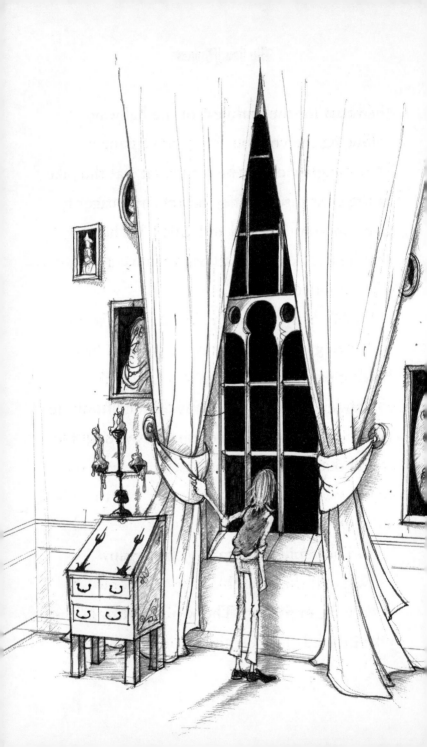

'What? I mean, pardon?'

'Stanley, listen. You are in grave danger. The Stormbringers are drawing near. Their frozen prison lies in pieces and they are heading south even as we speak, never stopping or resting, only ever moving forward until they get here.

'I shall send my greatest enemy to help you.'

'What? Pardon?'

But that was it. Silence was on the pike once more, and Stanley knew that no matter how he tried the pike would only speak when he felt the need. It might be days or weeks before he spoke again.

Stanley went back to the front room and looked out through the window at the pitch black of night. He slumped back into his chair and wrapped himself in his blanket.

He would try and get some sleep, but he knew it would be difficult now.

In the morning, Mrs Carelli was on the warpath straight away. 'Stanley! How come I has slept like a baby for six months in this big old place all alone since you left – and then as soon as you come back I can hear you wandering around in the night, up and down the hallway, mumbling away like some demented ghost! What's going on now? I thought we'd cleared up all our problems.'

Stanley could only stare, speechless and groggy through tiredness.

'Sorry,' he said. 'Sleepwalking! I'll stay in my room tonight.'

And so began Stanley's second visit to Crampton Rock. Mrs Carelli was already all over him like a rash – and, unless Stanley was very much mistaken, his friend the pike had greeted him with the news that he was in grave danger.

'Oh, and another thing,' Mrs Carelli continued. 'The fire needs cleaning out, the garden wants some help, and when you've done all that we're gonna have to start the winter decorating.'

She fired her orders at him like little arrows and he felt them pounding his head.

'Winter decorating? What's winter decorating?'

'You know, lad, winter jobs inside the house where it's warm and the paint can dry. There's the kitchen, the dining room and then there's a couple of rooms upstairs. This house won't grow arms and paint itself, young Buggles. You has to look after your inheritance.'

'Oh, yes, absolutely,' Stanley agreed. He wandered upstairs, climbed into his bed still clothed, and slept until midday.

The return
of the
Old Buccaneer.

Stanley fell into bed that night, worn out
by the day's exertions inside and outside
the house. But he was not destined to sleep
in peace.

The yellowy-white translucent light of a
long-dead and well-respected scoundrel
began to form by the side of Stanley's bed
until it was the fully formed (but headless)

figure of a man. Of course, Stanley was blissfully unaware of this. It was three in the morning and he was wrapped in his bedclothes preserving warmth and dreaming furiously.

The spirit began to grow impatient. He stamped his feet against the floorboards and paced up and down the room, feeling his way around, stumbling here and there. He knew the place well but it was still a task to find his way around with only his hands and feet.

Still nothing. The spirit felt for Stanley's sheets, and when he was sure he held them in his hand, he unrolled the tight chrysalis with a prompt jerk. Thrashing wildly, Stanley rolled on to the floor.

Finally, Stanley was awake ... but he felt sure that he must still be dreaming. He could feel the hard wood beneath him and something had very definitely and deliberately hurled him from his nest. (This was the bit that told him he was awake.) But in front of him was a headless man in a naval uniform and a long sword secured at his side.

Stanley's heart beat faster. He rubbed his eyes. But the longer he looked, the longer the headless man was still there, and it was becoming clear that what he could see wasn't anything to do with being half asleep. In fact, it had everything to do with being wide awake.

Stanley found himself shaking uncontrollably, and tried to calm himself with big deep breaths. His mother had always told him that there was an explanation for everything. Stanley had to conclude that the most reasonable explanation at the moment seemed to be that the house was haunted.

The figure was pointing to where it knew the door would be and gestured to him to move. Stanley felt he had no choice. When they reached the hallway, the headless man turned his finger downwards.

He wanted Stanley to head down the staircase. Stanley took great care to avoid all the creaking steps, although his knocking knees seemed to be making the most noise. He didn't want Mrs Carelli hearing the commotion. But his great care was demolished by his midnight partner, who thudded down the steps like an elephant, tripping on the carpet and losing a leg through the balustrades.

Finally reaching the ground floor, the spirit frogmarched Stanley through the house, using his hand to find his way along the walls and sending all the little paintings higgledy-piggledy.

They entered a room where there was a large portrait on the wall, and the headless man pointed to the name.

Admiral Swift

Then he stood beside it so that the head and face of the painting were on his shoulders.

'Oh my goodness. You're … you're Admiral Swift. You're Great-Uncle Bart!'

The spirit was unable to reply, of course, so he held out his hand to Stanley and shook it with a firm ghostly grip.

'Err … pleased to … meet you, Great-Uncle Bart!' Stanley announced, feeling slightly uneasy at the thought that he was shaking the hand of a man with no head in the freezing cold at the dead of night.

But ah well, who cares, he thought. He'd try anything once.

Admiral Swift kept hold of Stanley's hand, dragged him through to the front room and over to the window where the panes were so cold they were frosted on the inside. Stanley waited. His dead uncle lifted the forefinger of his right hand and drew four words, one inside each small square pane that ran along the bottom of the window.

I need my head

'Ahh,' said Stanley. 'I see. Well of course I'd like to help but, well … erm, the thing is, you see, that, well … erm.' And as he struggled to find the right words, his

Great-Uncle Bart faded slowly until there was nothing there at all. But Stanley knew that he had not seen the last of Admiral Swift.

He returned carefully to the warmth of his pit and studied his thoughts, tossing and turning until at last he found his way back into a deep sleep.

In Stanley's dream he saw the Admiral's head everywhere. Under the bed, in the cupboard, in the fireplace, under his old hat that still rested on the hat stand. He even saw it mounted on the wall in the hallway next to the old moose. One minute the head had glowing eyes. The next minute it had only *one* eye.

Then it was just a skull.
Then it was
laughing loudly
with its jaws wide open
and after that it was talking
away to Mrs Carelli on
the kitchen table
as she baked
bread.

And what on
earth would Mrs Carelli
do if she saw Admiral Swift wandering
around the house?

All of this had given Stanley a very disturbed
night, and his tired body would not allow
him to wake before lunch.

But when he woke, something had clicked
into place inside his head.

41

The pike had said he would send his greatest enemy to help Stanley.

Of course, Admiral Swift was the one who had fished the pike from the lake, ending his life, and had him preserved. So surely Admiral Swift must have been who the pike meant when he said he would send his greatest enemy.

Now it made sense. And in that case it meant that Great-Uncle Bart was here to help Stanley. To help him with the coming of the Stormbringers.

When Stanley finally emerged from his room, it was almost dark again. He looked out through the hallway window. The air was still freezing cold and low cloud hung over the harbour waiting to announce an early dusk. The boats had stayed still all day and the water looked unforgiving.

Stanley turned downstairs. He wanted to consult the pike, but was confronted by Mrs Carelli straight away.

'Ahh, here he is, look,' she said, smiling from one ear to the other. 'Come on, Stanley. Come and say hello. You got a guest!'

Stanley peered round the archway that led into the kitchen, half-expecting that his dream had come true and Admiral Swift's head would be perched on the table, talking away. But instead, there at the table sat a girl, about his own age.

Her eyes were a pale-blue wash and her little pupils seemed to stare right at him. Short tufts of cropped hair gave her the look of a young tearaway and she was dressed in ragged winter woollens with a pair of black fingerless gloves.

'This is the master of the house. Though you wouldn't think so to look at him, would you? Say hello, Stanley. This is Daisy. She's Mister Grouse's niece, from the lighthouse.'

'Oh, hello,' said Stanley. 'Pleased to meet you.' He stumbled over his words slightly and his face reddened as he held out his hand to shake hers.

'Hello, Stanley,' said Daisy, grinning widely as she greeted him. 'I've heard a lot about you. I wasn't here last summer so I thought I'd get in a winter visit. I was very sorry about your Great-Uncle Bart. He was a nice man.'

Mrs Carelli jumped in. 'Daisy used to help me clean here, didn't you, poppet.'

'Yes, I know this place very well, Stanley,' Daisy announced. He somehow felt that she was passing him a knowing look – but if she was, it was very subtle, and he told himself he was imagining things.

'Ah, I see,' muttered Stanley, not sure what to say.

'But I got a new helper now, haven't I, Stanley?' Mrs Carelli grimaced. 'Except he ain't much help when he can't get out of bed 'cause he's been running round the house all night,' she carried on, clipping the back of his head as she walked past him.

'Damn it,' said Stanley to himself. He'd thought he'd got away with it. He made his excuses and skulked off upstairs to straighten his hair.

'We need firewood, young Buggles, before you disappear again!' Mrs Carelli shouted after him.

'He's a good lad,' she whispered to Daisy. 'He's just … well. He's just a boy, isn't he. And, well … boys is boys, you know.'

Stanley was outside filling the basket when Daisy wandered out through the back door.

'I'll be seeing you later then, Stanley,' she said. 'It was good to meet you. You got a great place here.' And she wandered down the path with her hands tucked neatly into her pockets.

'Oh, yes. Ouch. Good to meet you, Daisy. Aahhhhh! Ouch. Ouch!' Stanley had dropped a log on his foot, and then the

whole basket, and now the logs were rolling down the path towards his new-found friend.

'Are you OK, Stanley?' Daisy asked politely, turning and picking up the wood.

'Erm, yes, I'm fine,' he smiled and they shared a shy chuckle.

'I like you, Stanley,' she said. 'You're funny.' And she trotted off down to the harbour, towards the lighthouse.

An hour later, Stanley was stoking the fire. The wood he had collected was burning away nicely, and his memory of the previous night was now far enough away for him to tell himself he had been dreaming.

That was, until he turned to the window and realized he was not alone in the room. Great-Uncle Bart was standing with his arms folded, tapping his foot impatiently.

The spirit could not speak a word, of course. Instead he pointed his finger to the writing that could still be seen on the window.

I need my head

Stanley felt a surge of prickles tingling down his spine as he looked at Admiral Swift. His headless figure would send Mrs Carelli into a screaming fit, he was sure. She had hit the roof when she'd seen a *spider*.

Admiral Swift lurched restlessly around the room. He found a patch of dust on top of the mantelpiece and wrote it again with his finger:

I NEED MY HEAD.

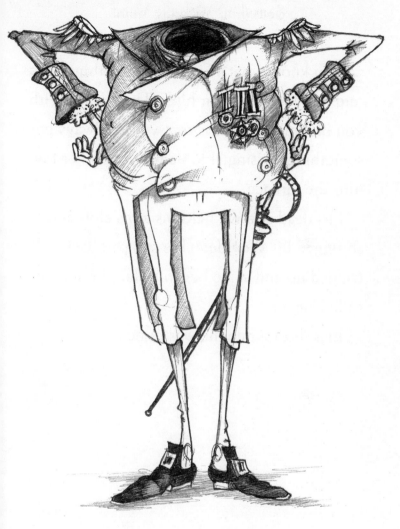

Stanley remembered the fingerless pirates from the summer who had forced him to shoot the werewolf.

'You know what? Can I say something?' said Stanley, hands on hips. 'The trouble with you bloomin' pirates is that you've always got something missing!' He slammed another log into the furnace.

His dead relative held his arms aloft and shrugged his shoulders. He stepped back, tripped up and as he began to fall, he started to fade again.

In a short while, he was gone.

A walk along the harbour

Stanley was meandering around, down at the harbour. It was somewhere he always liked to be. He'd thought he was alone, when he turned to see one bony half of a dead fish dangling in his face – and behind it a mischievous Daisy, grinning at him.

'Hungry?' she laughed.

'No thanks, I've eaten,' he said, straight-faced.

She threw the fish over the wall on to the sand.

'You look serious today!' she questioned, eyeing him closely. 'What's wrong?'

'How well did you know Admiral Swift?' he returned.

'Quite well,' she said. 'Why do you ask?'

'Would you like to meet him again?'

'Well, I guess so. But that's a fairly odd question, if you don't mind me saying so. After all, it's not really likely, is it?' she quizzed.

'Not as unlikely as you think, Daisy. There is something I need to tell you.'

Daisy stared at him expectantly, waiting for him to continue.

'I have had a visit … from Admiral Swift.'

Daisy narrowed her eyes, half-expecting that he was joking. But, studying his expression, she knew he was serious.

'I've seen some strange goings-on up at the Hall, Stanley, but I haven't ever seen anything I could describe as a ghost.'

'Well, I've seen one, and it belongs to Admiral Swift,' he insisted.

'What does he *want*, then?' she asked. Stanley noticed that she was trembling slightly, but she insisted that she was frozen, not frightened.

'They say that ghosts only appear when their souls are restless!' she continued. 'He must want something, Stanley.'

'He does. He wants his head.'

Daisy stared harder still, and before he knew it Stanley had told her everything.

'That's a lot to take in,' she admitted. 'But if you need my help, it's yours.'

Stanley thanked her, smiling swiftly then looking down at the sand. They carried on walking. The seabirds scattered as they drew nearer, and they watched a handful of fishermen dismantling a large sail from a boat.

'There's never a dull moment here, is there?' said Stanley with a grin, breaking the silence.

'Not when *you're* here!' she laughed, breaking into a run.

They spent a happy afternoon on the beach, splashing each other in the rock pools and Stanley chasing Daisy with scrag-ends of seaweed. Then they headed to the lighthouse, and Stanley called in to say hello to Mr and Mrs Grouse. When he left he was armed with a box full of whiting, a present for Mrs Carelli.

Daisy followed him to the lighthouse door

and they stood
outside together,
looking over the harbour.

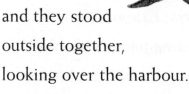

Stanley put on his best
funny voice and pulled his
face into a strange grimace.
He placed the lid of
the box on his
head and wore
it like a hat,
saluting Daisy.

'Very well,
captain,' he
began, 'I shall
return home. I will
report back within
twenty-four hours.
Permission to
leave, sir?'

'You may leave now, Corporal Buggles,' she announced, giggling uncontrollably as Stanley marched away, dropping fish as he went and being pounded by the seagulls.

The warriors marched onward, knee-deep in snow, down into the sinister darkness of the icy valleys. The harsh winter weather bit at their craggy faces and the wind whipped up the tails of their long coats, but they felt nothing. Nothing except the need to take what they felt was theirs, and take it soon.

A dreadful Task

When Stanley returned to the house, Mrs Carelli was down the corridor where the pike was hanging on the wall.

'This place is filthy! There's so much to dust and clean around here I can't get near the place. You make the meal tonight, young man, and I'll go about my jobs. Thank you.' She bobbed around the pike's glass case with a long feather implement, making funny little movements as she removed the layers of dust.

She stood back from it and gave it a scowl. 'You know something, lad, I think it's time we got rid of some of these old ornamentations and decorations.'

Stanley stopped and stared at her in a panic.

'I mean, will you take a look at that. Did you ever see such an ugly, useless, baggy old lifeless lump of a fish in all your days? If ever a beast was in need of an early retirement it's this one. What do you say, Stanley? Shall we give him a swim in the drink?'

'AHH, NO. NO WAY. Erm, I mean … well, actually, I do like it … a lot,' Stanley squealed.

'My goodness, Stanley. Touched a nerve there, didn't I? Had no idea you were so keen on the old trout.'

'Pike.'

'Begging your pardon, young man?'

'It's a *pike*, Mrs Carelli. And a very beautiful example at that, and I should be happy to keep it, thank you very much,' he insisted.

'All right, all right,' she said. 'Now get down from your high horse and go put your apron on.'

It was much, much later when Stanley had the chance to be alone with the pike again, and he had waited anxiously for the opportunity. He was standing in front of him and admiring his freshly dusted case when he finally spoke.

'Aaahh, young Master Buggles. I see you

have found it necessary to seek out my help
again. Or perhaps, like your housekeeper,
you simply wish to insult my appearance,'
he began.

'Ah … I'm sorry about
that. Mrs Carelli
means no harm,
I'm sure,' Stanley
explained.

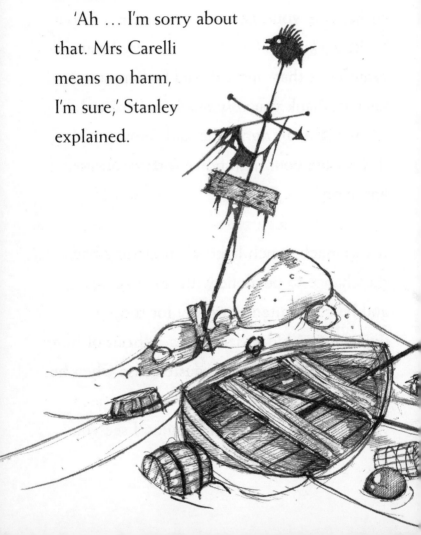

'Never mind. She has dusted my window and improved the view, so I shall forgive her.'

'I need your help,' started Stanley. 'I have had two visits from Admiral Swift, who I know you sent to help me – but he is without his head.'

'Yes, of course. First things first, my dear boy, first things first. I sense a little excursion for myself in all of this.

'Let me explain. Poor old Admiral Swift found out how it felt to be the victim of a predator – much as I did when he pulled me out of the lake and had me gutted. Still, I bear no grudge and I am here to help you, Stanley. You need your great-uncle badly, and he needs his head.

61

But his poor old noggin lies at the bottom of Crampton Springs. They are very deep and dangerous, I'm afraid – but I know an excellent swimmer who could spear down into the darkness and retrieve that watery lump.'

'You mean … yourself?'

'Ahhh, Stanley. You have the mind of a genius. Always thinking ahead.'

Stanley scratched his head. How could the pike swim, since he wasn't alive? But then again, how did the pike speak, since he wasn't alive? He did not like to ask an impertinent question; the poor old pike had heard enough insults for one day.

'And you said that I should be fearful because the Stormbringers are coming?' Stanley asked instead, taking his opportunity to put more questions to the pike while he could.

'So you should, Stanley. So you should,

for still they come. Through icy winds and rain and over hills and valleys they move. For many miles they have trekked, without stopping or resting. Through night and day they press on fearlessly.'

'But what does that *mean?*'

'I think your deceased great-uncle is the best person to explain all that, Stanley. Let us firstly deal with the retrieval of his head. I prefer to swim in the morning. Tomorrow will be fine. Thank you, Stanley. I shall see you then.'

The pike had made his mind up, and Stanley dared not challenge him.

Tomorrow would be an interesting day.

7

A fish out of Water

Outside, the cold had taken a firm grip over Crampton Rock. Stanley stared out from his bedroom window. Frost scratched at the panes, and an icy draught slipped in round the window frame. Stanley could feel in the air that it was about to snow heavily; a freezing wind was whipping up a storm in the distance.

And it was carrying something with it.

Stanley knew he had to be up early the next morning, and that alone was enough to give him a poor night's sleep, never mind all his other trials and troubles. By the time he saw Daisy again there would be so much more to tell her. And he wasn't sure she would even believe most of it.

At six a.m. he was unscrewing the pike's glass case, in the dark of the early morning. He placed it carefully on the floor.

And now for the pike. Stanley was almost afraid to touch him, and he was also worried about the safety of the Ibis. He knew that he must not touch it again. But just as he was thinking this very thought, the pike spoke.

'Take the tongs from the kitchen drawer, Stanley, and remove her carefully from inside me. Place her under the loose floorboard that

sits directly beneath
me. Don't be afraid.
I trust in you.'

Stanley felt
good. The pike
trusted him. But
when he fumbled at the
floorboards, he found himself unable to lift
them at all. Frustrated, he ran to the kitchen
and returned with the tongs and a sharp
blade that he used to ease up the edge of the
boarding.

'That's it,' encouraged the pike. 'She will
be fine resting there. We do not want to
waken every crook and villain from here to
eternity. You would not wish to start the
quickening – otherwise you can say goodbye
to all you have.'

Stanley was listening with the tongs in

his hand, waiting for the pike to finish. He knew nothing of this thing he called the quickening.

'You look confused, young Stanley,' continued the fish, 'but don't be. It is quite simple. When you held the Ibis in your hand, a faint quiver echoed across the earth. But if she touches the water, a monstrous tremor will waken the world of the dead and buried, and you will have to fight for your life.'

Stanley stared wide-eyed in disbelief, but deep down he knew that the pike had always told him the truth. He swallowed the lump in his throat.

'Now, take me in your arms and let us do what we need to do,' instructed the pike.

Cupping the fish's belly with his left hand, Stanley placed his right arm over his back, just in front of the large fin. At first it felt awkward, but then the pike seemed to wriggle right into place.

Oh, what a strange feeling. The sensation of holding the great fish was hypnotic, and Stanley felt himself swooning and buckling at the knees.

'Keep your head, little hero!' requested the pike.

Stanley gathered his thoughts and carefully made his way to the kitchen door. The fish was heavy, and he remembered the inscription on the casing: 'A preserved 22 1/2lb pike caught by Admiral Bartholomew Swift in Crampton Springs, 1827.' And the walk up to the lake was a lengthy one.

An icy blast assailed Stanley as he fumbled at the door. He set out into the morning with his scarf-wrapped head down, struggling to pull on his gloves as he held on to the pike's carcass. A trail of footprints outlined his path as he crunched across the frosted lawn towards the gate, to make his way across the moor.

As he walked he sang to cheer himself. The strange sensation of carrying the pike warmed him, but it grew heavier as he ventured further.

In a short while they were up by the old water mill, and when they had crossed the wooden footbridge he stopped to rest a while on a milestone.

'You are doing well, Stanley. It is cold for you I know, yet I do not feel it myself.' The pike felt a surge of excitement, and his belly tingled. He longed for the water.

Stanley did not answer. He was regaining his breath. Instead, he patted the head of the pike to acknowledge him, then he rose to his feet and carried on.

Unfortunately it was all uphill from there.

The journey had taken forty minutes
in the freezing cold. On a summer's day
Stanley would have trotted there in ten,
but at last he was at the edge of the lake.

'Ahhh, home again!' said the pike –
and for a second, Stanley wondered if it
was a good idea to let him back into the
water. But he hadn't come this far to
change his mind at the last minute, so he
braced himself over the water's edge.

'When you're ready, Stanley. When
you're ready.'

The great fish slithered downward into the
icy drink, and the last Stanley saw of him was
his tail flickering in a sharp sword-like move
that propelled him into the depths.

Stanley sat and waited for what seemed
like hours. He felt the ends of his stringy

hair freezing together in lumps as he
watched the morning light start to appear
over the sea.

Below, the pike glided gracefully. Oh, the
feeling was too good. I could stay here, he
thought. I would really be so much happier if
I was still here among the reeds.

He searched through the flowing tendrils of plants and watched the water life dart out of his way. Oh yes, they feared him. He was

really someone down here. Someone grand and respected. No one thought he was a *trout* down here. They knew the difference, and it meant a great deal to all of them.

Then he shot downwards into the deep. He was searching now. He knew the head of Admiral Swift would lie at the bottom, surrounded by shale and pebbles with its hair floating, web-like, in the swirl of the water. Then, out of the darkness, he glimpsed the milky-white skin of the Admiral's face. Deep down, he just wanted to nip off his nose and leave it there while he settled back in to life among the reeds. But Stanley needed him.

The pike took a good length of wispy white hair between his sharp teeth. Then, with a sharp flick that stirred up the silt from the bottom, he turned and pierced upwards towards the oncoming morning light.

And finally he was back.

As Stanley sat waiting, the pointed nose of
the pike and his glassy eyes suddenly
appeared beneath the water, then he rocketed
out and landed, THUMP, back into Stanley's
arms, nearly knocking him flying.

Something grey and grisly was held fast
between the pike's sharp teeth. It swayed
from side to side, spraying cold water, almost
unrecognizable at first, but
Stanley could soon see
that it was Admiral
Swift's head.

Stanley tried not to look at it too closely, and began striding back, to be done and dusted with this dreadful task. By the time he had reached the water mill, he could bring himself to take a quick glance at the face. Its eyes were shut and it seemed to be changing from pure white to ever so slightly purpley-blue. Stanley almost felt the urge to tell Admiral Swift he was looking a bit better.

He was making good progress and began to sing to himself again. But this time, he was joined by a nearby voice. Who could it be? He stopped and looked around. It was much lighter now, but he could see no one.

Stanley kept singing and the voice joined him again. He stopped and looked down. Admiral Swift was singing with him, keeping his eyes shut whilst he adjusted to the light. The pike could not open his mouth, for

he would drop the head, but he began to
hum along.

Stanley felt obliged to carry on and
though there was much nervousness in his
voice at the absurdity of it all, the three of
them made a wonderful sound through the
chilled morning air.

But as they crossed
the lawn the singing
was brought to an
abrupt end by a
puzzled Mrs
Carelli. She
stood
scratching
her head as
she opened
the door to
Stanley.

'For goodness' sake, Stanley, when I said we ought to drop him in the drink I didn't mean it! Where have you been with him? And what on earth are you doing out of your bed at this time of a morning, you skinny little lummox? You'll catch your death of cold. Anyway, I thought you wanted to keep him.'

She was rambling away to herself by this time and Stanley wasn't listening. He was too busy concealing the head of Admiral Swift beneath his coat in a panic. He knew that Mrs Carelli had seen plenty of things in her lifetime, but if she saw the head of Great-Uncle Bart she would keel over.

'… and why did you take him all the way out to sea and bring him back again? And why did you go out through the back gate?'

On she went, but Stanley was only relieved that she hadn't noticed the head.

'Erm, Mrs Carelli? I'm sorry, but could I just get back inside?' he asked. 'It's extremely cold.'

'Come on,' she said. 'Let's put your favourite old trout back on the wall and say no more about it, eh? No need for nonsense now, is there, Stanley? You put him back in his box and I'll fix you some breakfast. How about that?'

'OK,' said Stanley. As soon as it was safe, he slipped upstairs to his room and placed the Admiral's noggin under his bed.

Back downstairs, he found himself being eyed carefully by Mrs Carelli, almost as if she thought he was ill. He put the pike back in his case and thanked him, then went to devour his breakfast.

As Stanley sat over a bowl of steaming porridge, doing his best to convince Mrs Carelli that he was still quite normal,

Admiral Swift wandered into the kitchen. He stood just behind Mrs Carelli, trying to attach his head to his dumpy little frame. Just as in the painting, his great-uncle's head sunk into his shoulders and it appeared that he had no neck. Stanley stared in horror, his spoon held halfway up to his mouth. This was the first time he had seen his great-uncle in one piece.

Admiral Swift squeezed and pulled, twisted and turned. Stanley winced.

'*Now* what's the matter, Stanley? What are you staring at?' despaired Mrs Carelli.

But when she turned round, Admiral Swift had paced off quietly down the hallway, out of sight.

'Oh, er ... my porridge is too hot. I'm sorry ... I ... erm,' Stanley muttered.

'I'm getting worried about you, lad,' Mrs Carelli continued. 'I think this weather has given you some sort of bug or something.'

Just then, Stanley's great-uncle appeared again. He gazed into the small mirror inside the doorway, adjusting his neck-tie. He looked pleased with himself, as if he was happy that he had got his head to fit like it should.

'Maybe I should get the doctor out to you.

I don't think your mother would be too
happy if she thought I wasn't looking after
you properly!'

Mrs Carelli was busying herself around the
table as she spoke. She was not a woman who
could keep still very well.

'I'm fine,' Stanley insisted. 'I just need to
settle back in. Life is very different on
Crampton Rock.' He ate the rest of his
porridge in silence, as Admiral Swift slowly
faded from view. But he knew he would be
seeing him again.

Later, Stanley dried the pike and gave him
a good brush and polish. Then, with the
greatest of care, he replaced the Ibis.

'You know something, Stanley,' said the
pike as the tongs were inserted into his
throat, 'I have enjoyed myself thoroughly

82

today. I had quite forgotten how it feels to dart through the reeds and feel the rush of the water against my scales. That's what life is about. We could do that again some time perhaps, could we not?'

Then he fell asleep.

A word to the Wise

'Now listen carefully, Daisy, this is important. A lot has happened since I saw you yesterday.'

That afternoon, Stanley and Daisy were sitting in the front room, looking over the harbour. Stanley was desperate to explain the whole scenario with the pike and Admiral Swift that morning. The fire was roaring away as they sat by the window, entranced by the gently falling flakes of snow across the bay. Small drifts of white had gathered at the corners of the panes.

With his nerves rattling in his throat, Stanley began to tell Daisy all that had happened.

He knew he still had some way to go before he convinced her that all he had said was true.

But Daisy was distracted. Her wide eyes steered past him and over his shoulder, back towards the fire. She couldn't speak, but pointed, wordlessly.

Stanley turned around and there in front of the crackling, spitting flames stood Admiral Swift.

The spirit walked over to the window, gave a huge grin, and shook Stanley's hand. Then for the first time, he spoke.

'Thank you, Stanley. I owe you a great deal for what you have done for me. It is good to meet you at long last, and I am sorry you are landed in this terrible mess. You have already shown more bravery than I have seen in any seafaring man.'

The Admiral's voice was deep, and what Stanley's mother would have called posh. Not at all what I expected from a pirate, Stanley thought. His great-uncle's face was different now and had much more colour in it … although Stanley wasn't sure that the colour was entirely appropriate.

Admiral Swift turned to Daisy.

'Daisy, it is good to see you again. I know you have a good heart. Stanley may need your help, and you will need to summon up more bravery than you ever thought you had.'

Daisy smiled and though she trembled slightly, she did not fear the spirit that stood before her.

The Admiral wandered around the room a little. Daisy and Stanley stared at each other, not knowing quite what to say.

'You know this is no ordinary storm, Stanley, don't you?' the spirit said, walking back to the window.

'Well, actually, no I don't. Well, I mean, I know it's going to be a bad one but, well … I don't know any more than that, I suppose,' Stanley admitted.

'Well, let us say that there is more than snow in the blizzard gathering out there on the ocean.'

The Admiral drew closer. 'That storm, Stanley, is a sign. It signals the approach of the deadliest spirit known to the pirate world.

If there was ever any good that came from
you meeting Flynn and the old buccaneers it

is that it has, in part, prepared you for Bastabelle Partridge. And you can be sure that he is accompanied by Jackdaw McCormick.'

Stanley shivered. The names had a sinister edge to them. He held his breath, waiting for his Great-Uncle Bart to continue.

'You see, Stanley, the Ibis has caused many problems for many years. In some ways I would have been better without it. But I was foolish.

'Bastabelle Partridge is the man I took it from. But that was one fight in a long line of disputes over many years. Everybody thinks it belongs to them, Stanley. But the point is that originally it *really did* belong to the family. My family. *Your* family. At one time I really was a naval officer, but an attack from pirates left me wounded and the navy refused to help me.

I turned against them and everyone else, and became one of the rogues that I had despised. It is not a good story to tell young children.

'Partridge and McCormick are the Stormbringers. Once they were great tradesmen on the ocean, ferrying goods back and forth from South America. Successful, too. Partridge and McCormick was big business. But then they stumbled upon the Ibis, and their desire to keep it cost them dearly. They became a deadly and fearsome duo, but eventually I claimed it back.'

'How?' Daisy cut in quickly.

'Well, let us just say that though they were great swordsmen, I was better. I caught up with them in Norway, where they had fled from the gathering onslaught of villains desperate to get hold of the Ibis. And there I slayed them both, out on the ice, took what was mine and left them to their frozen graves. There they stayed, until you awoke them, Stanley.'

'Me. Oh yes, of course, I know, I'm very sorry. I understand now that when I touched the Ibis something happened, awaking the dead.'

'That's right. We must be careful, young fellow. The Ibis is best left where it is, out of reach and untouched. We would not want to start the quickening. Our task right now, Stanley, and you too, Daisy, is to prepare ourselves for the Stormbringers. We have a fight on our hands!' he announced, tapping his hand against the handle of the long slim blade tucked neatly at his side.

Then, and not for the first time, he slowly faded away into the dark.

Stanley no longer had to convince Daisy of Admiral Swift's existence.

They walked to the door, chatting quietly, and she ran off down to the lighthouse before it got dark.

That night, Stanley climbed down from his bed and walked to the window. He stared out to sea. The snow was falling heavily and there was something very strange about the white snowflake sky at the black of night.

A glowing twisting whirlwind was just becoming visible on the horizon.

Partridge
and
McCormick

The snow lay thick upon the ground next morning. The fishing boats were stranded and Stanley wished that just for once he could enjoy the beautiful peace of a picturesque Crampton Rock without having to worry about what was around the corner.

Despite his worries, Stanley could not resist a dash around in the snow.

He ran over the hill to where the town gibbet stood, the dangling skeleton in his iron cage. The poor soul's skull was crowned with what looked like a peak of white meringue and looked so cheerful that Stanley laughed out loud.

Daisy appeared from the lighthouse. She was wrapped up to the eyes and threw snow in the air as she ran towards him. They reeled with laughter as they pounded each other with snowballs.

Finally exhausted, they walked down to the harbour and perched inside the cabin of a fishing boat where it was dry. They blew on their hands to warm themselves and when he had caught his breath a little,

Stanley recalled Admiral Swift's tale about the coming of the Stormbringers.

'It is only a matter of time before they're here,' he said. 'Great-Uncle Bart is right, I will need your help. I hope you're prepared, Daisy!'

'I guess so,' she conceded. 'But I don't like the sound of Partridge and McCormick.'

'Neither do I,' shuddered Stanley. 'Come on,' he said, desperate to forget his troubles. 'I'll race you on to the moor.'

They discovered some old wooden panels that lay discarded around the disused water mill. And they sledged downhill until the light was almost dropping again and they were sore with so much belly laughter. They were ready to head back when Daisy slid headlong into the undergrowth. Something dug deep into her shin bone and she winced

in pain. She sat up and, taking the sharp
thing in her hand, she
inspected it closely.

Stanley came nearer,
eyes wide open.

'That's a *tooth*,' he claimed.

'Sheep?' asked Daisy.

'No,' he insisted. 'It's canine, and it's way
too big for a sheep, anyway.'

She handed it to him. He held it between
his index finger and thumb and stared at it.
'Do you know what, Daisy, I think you've
found something very significant,' he
announced. 'This is so big, it must be from
the mouth of our dear friend the wolf. Well
done,' he smiled.

The tooth was long and sharp and pearly
white. 'Finders keepers,' he said. 'Here, don't
lose it.' And he carefully handed it back to

her. She wrapped an oak leaf around it and placed it in her pocket as Stanley pulled her to her feet.

The storm was whipping up more wind and the bleak moor was clearly the wrong place to be. They decided that if they didn't make their way back soon they would encounter real trouble. The moor was a deadly place in the wrong kind of weather, and they had ventured too far out. They set their sights for home.

As they struggled through the freezing gale, a creaking, rattling sound came up behind them. When they turned to look, a black carriage had pulled up beside them. The door was already open.

'Step inside, my dears, or you'll be buried under that blizzard within the hour,' came a voice.

Stanley and Daisy were eager to be out of the cold, but they hesitated. It was dark inside the carriage, too dark to see clearly, and a foisty smell hit them from within.

'Ahh, you are lucky this time, children. It is unfortunate to be caught out in such a

storm. A good job my friend and I were passing your way.'

The moor was a strange place for a carriage to be, and Stanley felt he must refuse the offer.

He could only just make out the face of the man who sat inside, large and wide and bearded. Something was strapped to his back and he appeared to be uncomfortable in his seat, squashing his friend into the corner. His voice was deep and low, yet somehow gentle.

'Come, come, my dears, you would be foolish to try and make it home alone, would you not?' the man said, as the carriage rocked in the blowing gale and snow pushed in through the windows.

Stanley detected a hint of frustration in the stranger's voice, which made him even more adamant that it would be unwise to join him.

'Thank you ever so much, sir, but we are almost home now. We will manage.'

'It's a good walk to the Hall, even from here,' the man pressured. 'Come on, jump in.'

'How do you know we're heading for the Hall?'

'My dear boy, an old sea dog like me doesn't miss much,' said the man. 'You're young Buggles, aren't you? Isn't it you that inherited the old place from your great-uncle? Excellent navy man, your great-uncle was, Stanley. Impeccable record. A great swordsman. And who is this pretty little thing then?'

'Daisy,' she replied shyly. 'Daisy Grouse. I'm staying with my uncle at the lighthouse.'

'Ah, of course, dear old Mister Grouse. Well, well, well. We *are* in distinguished company, are we not?' But still the man at his side made no sound.

'And ... I'm sorry, what was your name, sir?' enquired Stanley politely.

'Oh, you'll know me only too well before

long, young Buggles. I won't say my name until the next time we meet – in case you tire of hearing it,' he replied, laughing a deep laugh. He opened the door for them both and held out his hand to lead them in.

Stanley didn't like it. He was too pushy.

'Er … well, thank you, sir. It's most kind of you, but …' He pushed the handle back to secure it fastened again. And as he did so a covering of snow shook itself from the carriage door. A coat of arms was revealed, with a name plaque that betrayed the identity of the passengers on board. It was an intricately decorated piece, but that did not disguise the fact that it was skulled and crossboned. And on it were the following words:

Partridge and McCormick

PARTRIDGE & McCORMICK

Stanley reeled in horror. He grabbed Daisy awkwardly by the arm and pulled her along as he bolted into the safety of the whirling white wind. He was sure that the men would open the carriage door and try to follow them but for all the life in him, he could not bring himself to turn and look back.

When they finally reached the house, panting in exhaustion, the black carriage was standing in wait by the stone pillars at the end of the drive.

'It's them!' cried Daisy.

There were voices. Close angry voices. It was Partridge and McCormick, Stanley was sure of that. One was shouting at the other in anger and frustration and soon they could be heard arguing and fighting among themselves about what was the best way to deal with the children.

Now it was Daisy's turn to lead the way. She took hold of Stanley's hand as they ventured back on to the moor, and around to the back of the house, sneaking in through the garden gate and heading across the lawn. The back door was locked.

'Quick,' said Daisy, 'in here.' She lifted a small trapdoor next to the house and pulled him down into it. They sailed down a short chute into a pile of logs and coal.

'Where is this?' asked Stanley, bemused.

'It's the old fuel store,' explained Daisy as she brushed herself down. 'It's not used any more, not since Admiral Swift blocked off the access to the back of the house. Quite handy, though – it comes out into the kitchen. Good job it was open! You'd better put that bolt on, though,' she told him.

Stanley stared at her, taken aback. She really did know the house, even better than he did. He was reminded of just how big the old place really was and how much more there was to get to know. If only he could find the time!

They sneaked into the house, leaving a trail of sooty wet prints, and slunk up to the front window in time to see the carriage slowly moving out of sight.

It looked like, just for now, they were safe.

An unfortunate ending

Stanley's head was banging with all the worries that were upon him. He didn't need extra troubles, but as he stumbled through to the hallway he was confronted by Mrs Carelli. She was holding several tins of paint and a stack of brand-spanking-new brushes.

'That lot should keep you busy, young fellow,' she called to him. 'Mister Grouse has just called to take Daisy back home, so I thought you might need something to break the boredom.'

'Boredom!' Stanley gasped. He would give anything just to be bored.

Stanley was eager to tell Admiral Swift, if only he would appear, that he had come face to face with Bastabelle Partridge and Jackdaw McCormick.

Later, he sat around a warm fire with Mrs Carelli. She had warmed him through with a large hot meal on his return from the moor, and he was too tired to be bothered by piracy or any other such nonsense.

Suddenly, there was Admiral Swift, sitting next to Mrs Carelli. She was happily unaware, her eyes shut and her hands clasped across her middle, taking in the heat from the fire.

'Dear oh dear, Stanley,' began the Admiral.
'I feel you may have had a close shave with
our friends already. You have left me feeling
slightly concerned – though, I must admit,
you were on your toes.'

Stanley eyeballed Mrs Carelli. He watched
her chest gently rising and falling. She had
dropped off.

'Was it really them?' he whispered.

'Well, yes. Absolutely,' the spirit confirmed,
with one raised eyebrow.

'But he seemed friendly. He wasn't at all
what I expected.'

'Of course he wasn't, Stanley. Of course he
wasn't. That is his way of luring you into his
trap. *Step into my parlour, said the spider to the fly.*
Something tells me that when you met *me* I
was not what you expected either?'

'Maybe,' Stanley answered, staring at his feet.

'Then you must learn your lesson, Stanley. You must not let your preconceptions fool you. Mister Partridge is a slippery customer. He has a certain way of doing business, very different to Mister Flynn and friends. Now, if you'll excuse me, I shall go and practise my fencing skills.'

'Wait!' said Stanley. He had wanted to quiz his great-uncle further. But no, he was gone.

And then one eye opened and Mrs Carelli's voice came. 'Stanley, are you talking to yourself? I'm gonna get Doctor Peebles over to you, sharpish. I'm sure you got a fever, lad.'

'I'm fine!' he insisted. 'I'm fine.'

Night drew in quickly. The snow and wind were relentless and the temperature dropped even lower.

That night was to be the most dreadful

110

night Stanley had ever experienced. Even worse than the night he had been forced to go out on to the moor and be rid of the werewolf.

The snow was piling up in a way that Stanley had never seen before. Thick drifts caused by the winds swept up the sides of buildings and into corners, bringing the roofs closer to the ground.

Stanley sat watching it come down from his bedroom window. The lights were off and it was late. Mrs Carelli's snoring echoed down the corridor, announcing that she was soundly asleep.

Crampton Rock looked desolate in the darkness. No one had been in the look-out posts for some time.

Stanley sensed something was behind him and when he turned round Admiral Swift was sat on his bed.

'I wish you wouldn't do that!' squeaked Stanley. 'You frightened me half to death. I thought it was *them*.'

Admiral Swift leaned forward and stood himself up.

'Listen, Stanley, and listen carefully. You may not see me after tonight.'

'I beg your pardon?'

'Tonight I will enter into a battle to protect what belongs to you and to the family. Bastabelle Partridge is on his way here again right now and he wants only one thing. We mustn't let go of it, Stanley.

'In a short while I will refuse to hand over the Ibis, and I will then engage in combat with my greatest enemy. I killed him before, but I need to prepare you in case this time I meet my end. When a spirit is killed by another spirit, he dies out for ever. That is the way it is. I cannot change it.'

'That's dreadful!' gasped Stanley. 'Let's be rid of the Ibis, so we can all live in peace on Crampton Rock. You don't have to fight. We can solve the problem for ever. Just – give it to him.'

'NEVER,' the Admiral huffed. 'No one shall ever put enough fear in me to force me into submission.'

And Stanley saw a swift glimpse of the bold, brave pirate that dwelled inside his great-uncle.

'Come, Stanley. Like I said, in case anything happens to me I need you to be prepared. Follow me.'

Stanley followed his great-uncle down the staircase and in a moment they were in front of the pike again.

'I do hope Admiral Swift isn't going to be foolish enough to take hold of the precious Ibis?' came the voice of the pike.

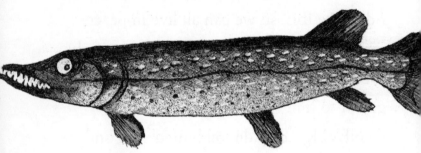

'Stanley, could you fetch me some tongs? They are in the kitchen drawer.' Admiral Swift asked.

Stanley did so and when he returned, the front of the glass case had already been removed and was resting on the floor. Admiral Swift placed the tongs carefully inside and curled them around the Ibis. Retrieving it, he held it up to where the moonlight shone in from the hallway window.

It was beautiful. Every colour he could think of seemed to show on its silvery surface.

'There is good reason for me showing you this again, young fellow. Something you haven't yet discovered.'

The Admiral turned it over, and at the back of it were two interlocking segments. He took out his sword and gently used the tip to flick the segments upwards, so they stuck out like prongs.

'There you go,' he said. 'It still works.'

'What do you mean, it still works?' quizzed Stanley.

'The Ibis is a key, Stanley. These prongs are made to push into two small holes. You see, the Ibis is only a part of something much more valuable: a casket crafted from silver. Needless to say, an ancient and valuable casket. It houses three keys below its lid: two of them, the Bison and the Jackal, are in place. The third, of course, is the Ibis. No one knows where the casket is, but the pirate world knows that the Ibis is the missing link. I don't think giving the Ibis away would stop those scoundrels from darkening your door, Stanley. All eyes would be on this place, because they think that the casket is here also.'

Stanley felt a leap of excitement, contained by his concern that he was into something dark and dangerous. He could see no way out of it.

'I saw her once,' the Admiral continued.
'Beautiful, she is. Pure silver, with the same
cascade of colours as the Ibis when the light
is on her, and wonderfully crafted. Only
small, yet big enough to house comfortably
what she conceals behind her closed lid. I do
not know exactly where she is, but many
think that the Ibis and the casket are close to
each other. I cannot say if that is true.'

'When was this? When you saw the casket,
I mean?'

'Oh, many years ago, Stanley. That is
another story. Perhaps when we have more
time I will tell you it.'

'And what is the secret she holds behind
her closed lid?' begged Stanley.

'Aah, now even I haven't got that far. And
if you ever do, then you have my blessing
and I wish you every ounce of luck.'

The Admiral placed the Ibis carefully down the throat of the pike and put the case back in position.

'Ah, such gentle hands,' said the pike. 'I wish you had been as careful when you took the hook from my lip. Still it hurts, even now.'

Stanley's great-uncle turned to look at him. 'Some people become bitter as they grow older, Stanley,' he smiled. 'Whatever you do in your life, don't grow old and bitter.'

'People?' questioned the pike. *'People?* I am not a person. I am a pike.'

'Mrs Carelli thinks you are a trout,' said Admiral Swift.

'There is only one old trout in this place,' the pike returned. 'And I think she fits the description better than I do.'

And that was all he would say before he returned to sleep.

'He has never forgiven me,' said the Admiral, 'and he would not have retrieved my head if he hadn't wanted to help you. You have a good friend in him, Stanley. He likes you.'

Stanley smiled. It felt strange to think of a preserved fish in a glass case as a good friend, but he did not say that out loud. He would never do that.

They returned to Stanley's room and sat in wait. It was a long vigil, and every minute seemed like an hour. Stanley must have peered from the window a thousand times as his great-uncle paced up and down the room. Every so often Admiral Swift would whip out his sword and take a slice at the empty space in front of him. Then he would put the sword back by his side and say in his best voice,

'And that is why they call me Swift.'

At almost three in the morning, the black carriage finally rolled up under the window. The Admiral shook Stanley's hand.

'Wish me luck,' he sighed. 'Don't come out. It's cold and there's nothing you can do. This is a clash of spiritual swords, my friend, and the best man will win.'

Then he was gone. A tear welled up in Stanley's eye. What if he never saw his great-uncle again?

Stanley was almost too scared to look from his window, yet somehow he *had* to look.

Admiral Swift was standing outside the carriage. Bastabelle Partridge opened the door and stepped out. He was huge, almost square, with a great black beard that cascaded down his front, and he seemed to be alone. To Stanley's surprise, when the pirate approached Admiral Swift he shook his hand and they spoke politely to each other.

Then he was just as surprised when Partridge whipped out his sword – and in a flash they were battling blades in the snow. Admiral Swift denied his old age and moved around in a wick fashion, twisting and turning. What a professional. Partridge was quick, despite his monstrous frame, but Swift was moving too fast and took a sly slice at his opponent's middle, wounding him badly.

But Partridge would not give up and forced himself to keep going, clutching his wound with his free hand.

They danced around the black carriage, crossing their blades as the snow and wind whirled around them. And then suddenly, in a flash of a movement, Swift had Partridge right where he wanted him. The Admiral was backed up against the carriage door, but Partridge had dropped his sword and Swift had his piercingly sharp blade perched under Bastabelle's chin.

The two of them were still and silent. This was it.

The very moment had arrived.

Partridge grinned a wide grin. Stanley thought he looked extremely calm, considering he was about to say goodbye to the world of wandering spirits.

And if only Admiral Swift had made the move a second earlier, it would have been goodbye – but he hesitated.

And in that moment's hesitation, Swift found that Partridge was not alone after all.

Jackdaw McCormick was right behind the very door the Admiral was backed up against. Like the sting of a bee, McCormick's blade shot through the carriage door and straight through Admiral Swift.

That was all it took. Bastabelle Partridge stayed right where he was, and watched as Admiral Swift dropped to his knees and then fell flat on his face.

And that, I am afraid to say, was the end of Admiral Swift.

Stanley watched in horror. As he looked through the frosted panes of his window, the flickering coloured light of the Admiral's spirit soared upward into the falling flakes and petered out towards the stars. He was gone for ever. Not far away, in the churchyard where he had been buried, his headstone cracked and crumbled to the ground in a million pieces.

Right there and then, Stanley's shock and horror was overshadowed by the terrible danger. There was no Admiral Swift to look over the house any more, and the evil figure of Partridge stood by the door to the Hall.

But Stanley had one stroke of luck. Admiral Swift had managed to wound his enemy, and he could not stand without the aid of his long-legged sidekick McCormick. They hobbled pathetically into the coach, cursing loud enough to reach Stanley's window, that they would return. The blackened shape of the carriage disappeared into the night.

Stanley was wrapped in grief. He had barely got to know his great-uncle, and now it was all over. He could not turn to Mrs Carelli. She knew nothing of this and she would think him mad.

He stood staring from his room across the harbour and the tears cascaded down his face.

The snow was piling up and he watched from his bed until all he could see was white. Then he fell asleep.

11

A touch of Magic

At daybreak, Stanley ran to the lighthouse
and beat at the door until Daisy appeared.
He was shaken by the death of his great-
uncle, and desperate for Daisy to know of the
danger they would be in as soon as Partridge
returned.

Daisy didn't know what to do for the best.
She agreed to come back to the Hall with

him, and they sat for hours talking of plans and plots. It was no easy task.

Eventually Stanley fell asleep on his bed, weary after his long night.

Daisy wandered across the hallway into the room opposite. They had spent much time in here: it was home to a host of ancient books and papers, and the drawers and cupboards were filled to the brim with every kind of weird and wonderful object. Birds' eggs, butterflies, insects and spiders, all neatly labelled. Jars and bottles of colourful potions and lotions that had stood for years unused.

'Surely *something* here will help,' said Daisy to herself. She searched alone as Stanley slept, rooting through the parchments and papers and delving deep into the sinister contents of long-untouched manuscripts.

In a corner, propping up the broken leg of a small table, was a large book with a black cover. It had an intricately scribbled title: *Notes and Notions*.

Inside it were endless notes in elaborate handwriting – strange ideas, spells and magic filled the pages. Little drawings peppered the corners and spaces between the paragraphs. Daisy searched and searched.

She was interrupted by Mrs Carelli. 'Ah, there you are, poppet. I think you should stay here tonight.' The weather had grown so foul that even the short walk to the lighthouse was treacherous, and Mrs Carelli had already shouted down to one of the villagers at the harbour to call on Mr Grouse and tell him she was safe and warm for the night.

Little did Daisy know what a terrifying ordeal it would be.

Daisy was just down the corridor from Stanley, in a large room with a huge bed that had been unoccupied for almost as long as it had been in Candlestick Hall. She couldn't see the sea, but the window overlooked the churchyard and it was postcard-pretty under a crispy white covering.

She had placed the black book in her room, with the intention of reading it that night, clinging to the hope that she would find the answer she needed between its damp and foisty pages.

Late that night, sleepily turning over yet another page, she was confronted with a short passage headed: '*Life and death and back again*'. She read it through once or twice, then folded the corner of the page so that she could find it again. Soon after, she fell asleep, the book still laid out in front of her.

Some time further into the early hours, Stanley awoke from a light sleep and thought he heard something moving. He felt sure that there was movement in the corridor.

His door creaked and his heart leaped as he watched the gap open and a face stare in at him from the blackness.

'Stanley, are you awake?'

Thank goodness. It was Daisy.

'Yes,' he answered. 'What's wrong?'

'Come and take a look from my window, quickly.'

Stanley fired into action. He half-knew what to expect, and threw clothes over his nightwear as he went. They turned into Daisy's room and drew close to the window.

Together they watched as the black carriage came into view, wading through the drifts. It was silent as it went, but the wind whipped up around it like a tornado.

The coach moved awkwardly, its huge bulk leaving a deep furrowed trail behind it, gliding right under their window. It almost disappeared out of sight as Daisy and Stanley pushed their frozen faces up to the glass to see where it had stopped.

'The eye of the storm is here, Daisy. *This is it*. Somehow we are going to have to deal with this … But I don't know where to start!'

Stanley didn't have to wait long. A smash of glass came from the dining hall, followed

by a horrendous thud and crack. He and Daisy ran down the corridor and headed down the long staircase, bursting into the room.

A huge cannonball had been hurled through the window, splitting the grand table clean in two. The icy snow blew in through the gap, intruding into the warmth of the house.

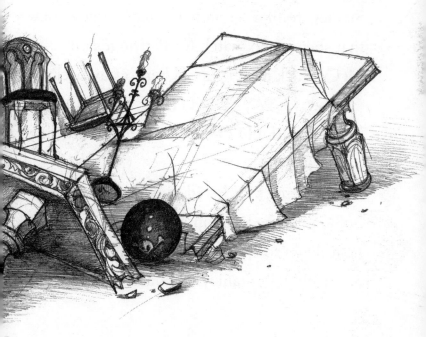

Through the darkness, a fat silhouette was forcing itself through the broken glass and pulling on the long drapes.

But it wasn't just Daisy and Stanley who'd been woken by the noise.

'GET YOUR FILTHY STINKIN' HANDS OFF MY BEST CURTAINS, YOU BIG LOUSY LUMMOX!'

Mrs Carelli bustled up behind Daisy and Stanley, rolling pin in hand. But Stanley knew that she was no match for Partridge and McCormick and he urged her to stay back.

'YOU'LL PAY FOR THOSE WINDOWS, YOU BEARDED OAF!' she cried as Partridge came closer.

McCormick slithered in behind his friend, holding a long weapon close to his chest. He bent down to speak to Mrs Carelli. He was massively tall: Stanley reckoned he must have been eight feet in height, and his face was desperately unpleasant. A patch covered his left eye and his long slope of a nose matched the contours of his chin.

Stanley knew right there and then that Jackdaw McCormick had never had a good bone in his body for as long as he'd lived.

'Now, now, miss. Let us not lose our heads. We don't all want to end up like Admiral Swift now, do we?' sneered Jackdaw.

Mrs Carelli *really* didn't like that. In a burst of temper, she lunged forward at him, but he was way too powerful and batted her off like a fly. He sent her hurtling into the corner of the room, where she lay gasping for breath.

Stanley and Daisy ran to her and held on to her.

McCormick let out a sinister cackle, and Stanley would have loved to punch him square in the teeth.

Partridge carried on as if nothing had happened, dusting himself down as he came nearer.

'I'm very sorry about Great-Uncle Bart, Stanley. He was a noble man – but I'm afraid our differences had become too great. No one lasts for ever, my dear. It was a fair fight but a tough one and now I bear a scar to prove it.' He pulled his coat aside and revealed his horrendous wound to Stanley.

Stanley didn't answer. He just stared and waited for the next sentence from the man who always made himself sound reasonable, whatever he was saying.

'There is only the small matter of the Ibis to be dealt with, and we can be on our way,' Partridge continued. 'This weather will cease, and you can all get back to normal. How does that sound? I know it's here. I can feel it,' he said in a very matter-of-fact voice.

'I don't know what you are talking about,' Stanley said, shrugging his shoulders.

Partridge leaned forward so that Stanley could see each hair on his face. He grabbed Stanley's coat and pulled it close, bringing the boy with it.

The old pirate smelled disgusting – a most horrible whiff of ancient rotting bones and putrid flesh. 'Listen to me, young fellow. When someone placed the Ibis in their hand I'd been asleep for thirty years. I travelled three thousand miles along with Mister McCormick here to come and take what is rightly mine. So let us not enter into lies and tall tales that don't make sense. There's a good lad.' He let go, patted Stanley on the head and ruffled his long hair.

'I can feel the beating heart of that precious little bird. I know she is near, Stanley. Think carefully. Don't go losing everything you have for the sake of something you don't even need.'

Stanley knew that he was more at risk than he had been with

Flynn and the others. There was something
far more dangerous and cut-throat about
Partridge and McCormick.

Partridge stepped out into the hallway as
Stanley and Daisy helped Mrs Carelli to her
feet. Stanley had never seen her looking so
crestfallen. They had really knocked the wind
out of her sails, and he held on to her tightly
in a bid to protect her.

The Stormbringers crunched their feet over
broken glass and their snow-caked clothes left
muddy water dripping everywhere.

McCormick pushed past Stanley, grinning
as he lifted his patch to reveal a spookily
empty socket. Stanley jumped sideways.

'Thank you kindly,' McCormick sneered.
His lolloping frame hung awkwardly out of
shabby clothes, and his enormous hands and
feet seemed too big for his body.

He carried a cudgel that looked like it had done some damage in the past.

'It is somewhere here,' Partridge whispered. In seconds he had found the pike and stood in front of it, his eyes closed, as if in a trance. 'Here, Mister McCormick, she lies here, behind this case.'

Before Stanley could say anything, Partridge took hold of the case and pulled it clean away from the wall, bringing dust and rubble down on himself and not caring one bit.

'No, it's here. In my hands,' he announced. 'I feel it.'

The pike's eyes opened wider, in shock, but he did not speak a word. His instinct was to dart away through the water, but alas, it was not possible.

Partridge made his way to the front door with his friend in tow.

'We have what we were looking for, Mister McCormick. Now that was quite simple, wasn't it, Stanley? Thank you for your hospitality. I do hope to see you again, my dears.'

He made his way outside, leaving the door wide open for the blizzard to come sweeping in.

As McCormick turned to leave, he grabbed Stanley by his waistcoat and lifted him up with one hand till they were face to face. He smelled just as bad as, if not worse than, old Partridge. 'If you ever try to cross Partridge and McCormick again, young Buggles, I will squash you like a fly.'

An overwhelming rush of anger surged through Stanley. Who on earth did this long-legged louse think he was? His right arm was crushed against the door, but he raised his left and landed the sweetest hook right into McCormick's only eye.

'Aaaarrrrgh!'

McCormick dropped Stanley immediately, wailing in pain. He took his cudgel and swung it blindly as tears leaked from under his eyelid.

Stanley dodged and the nail on the end of the weapon embedded itself in the doorframe, leaving the cudgel stuck in midair.

Partridge had seen the tussle, but his hands were not free and he was growing impatient. 'Come now, Mister McCormick. We have what we need. Let us not waste our energy on extending the battle we have already won.'

McCormick cursed at Stanley and made his way blindly outside, holding on to the coat tails of Bastabelle Partridge.

They climbed into the carriage, snow blowing into their faces. Partridge shouted in foul temper at the black mare and they bolted up on to the moor.

Stanley, Daisy and Mrs Carelli stood breathless in the doorway, the blizzard spinning around them, as the carriage moved off. Finally they dragged themselves away and forced the door shut against the storm.

Back inside they shook with fear and fever. Their bones were frozen to the core and they perched in front of the hearth to catch the last of the heat from the embers.

'Who on earth were they?' asked Mrs Carelli, nursing her injuries and shaking like a leaf.

'I'm afraid that they were more old enemies of Admiral Swift's,' said Daisy.

'But what did they want with Stanley's sardine?' she quizzed.

Stanley promised he would explain in the morning but that right now he felt that she should be wrapped up in bed. She would be sore when she woke and would need a day of rest.

Daisy and Stanley hurried her upstairs and made her comfortable – and for once Stanley felt good that he had taken charge. But when he was sure she was fine for the night, he climbed back into his woollens. As he headed out of the door, Daisy was close behind. It was bitterly cold but they were both moving so fast they were sweating profusely.

Daisy caught up with Stanley. 'Can you see them yet?' she asked.

'No, but I've picked up the tracks and they're heading this way.'

They pressed on together. 'What are we going to do, Stanley? They're too powerful for us.'

'Let's worry about that when we get there,'
Stanley said. His brow was knitted: what
grated on him the most was not the loss of
the Ibis, but the way McCormick had treated
Mrs Carelli. Stanley was hell bent on
revenge, on something far more punishing
than a sock in the eye.

Back inside Candlestick Hall, Mrs Carelli felt
sure that Stanley had crept out. She knew
him too well. She pulled her aching body
from the bed and wandered down the
corridor. Perhaps she was mistaken, and they
were in their beds after all. But no, Daisy's
room was empty and so was Stanley's.

Mrs Carelli walked from room to room,
looking out through the windows and trying
to catch a glimpse of them. Finally she
reached Daisy's room again, strained to see

out through the snow, then groaned at the pain in her side. She collapsed on the bed and gave a huge sigh. 'That boy will be the end of me,' she gasped.

She lit the candle that was perched on the small cabinet beside the bed and spotted the book Daisy had been reading before she went to sleep. At the top of the page, in a hand-written script, she read: '*Life and death and back again*'. Mrs Carelli knew those kids had been up to something. But this just sounded like nonsense! She read on, glancing through the endless notes and diagrams. She had no fascination for the subject, yet something made her continue.

Suddenly, out on the moor, Daisy glimpsed the black shape of the carriage ahead. Stanley's heart leaped. They had reached the

top of a hill, and from their lofty viewpoint
they could see the coach twisting and
winding, struggling in the snow.

The carriage lurched forward: a front
wheel had bashed into a snow-covered
boulder! It came reeling off and fell
in pieces to the ground,
spokes everywhere.

'Aha,' gasped
Stanley. 'A stroke
of luck! Come on,
Daisy, there must
be a way for
us to win this
battle.'

Daisy pulled
her hat down
over her
forehead

and shoved her freezing hands deep into her pockets. Something jabbed at her hand and she took it out.

It was the tooth that she had found out on the moor. She wrapped her fingers around it and held on tight. Perhaps it would bring them luck.

They drew nearer. They could see Bastabelle Partridge, enraged. McCormick was fumbling around trying to fix the wheel, but all to no avail.

Partridge began to unfasten the horse.

'Quick, Daisy, look. They're going to get away!'

Daisy held the tooth more tightly, so tightly that it almost cut into her hand.

Back at the Hall, leafing through the book, Mrs Carelli came across a passage decorated with silver swirls. Almost in a trance, she read out loud to herself:

By grip of claw
or hair or bone,

And with these words
outspoke alone,

Through icy blizzard wind of east
will tread the blackened midnight beast.

And as she spoke the words, a terrible gust took the page and whipped it out from the book, whisking it out through the window.

'Aah, these blasted windows need seeing to as well,' cried Mrs Carelli. She slammed the book shut. 'Wait till I get my hands on that pair of ruffians!'

Her candle flickered out, and the page flew across the moor.

Even the mighty Partridge was struggling to withstand the gale that was blowing up. His mare was spooked by the storm and, breaking free of the coach, bolted across the moor. The pirates' chance of a quick escape had just disappeared.

'Wait, Stanley, something is … happening,' said Daisy.

'What do you mean?' said Stanley, hopping from foot to foot in confusion.

'I don't know!'

They ran for refuge behind a huge rock, and not a moment too soon. A strange light was circling the ground before them. A cracking and sparking began, followed by a clap of thunder.

Suddenly, the hulking frame of a werewolf was appearing right in front of them through a whirling mist. The very werewolf that Stanley had defeated all those months ago.

The two friends were so frightened that they couldn't move a muscle.

Through his terror, Stanley looked into the wolf's eyes.

Something was different.

Daisy managed to whisper, 'Stanley, *run*! Run as fast as you can.'

But Stanley found that he was no longer afraid. Surely, if the wolf had wanted to savage them it could already have done so.

'No,' he hissed. 'Stay right there.' He grabbed the sleeve of Daisy's coat. 'Don't move an inch.'

Stanley crept closer to the beast, so close that he could see the scar left by his very own silver bullet. Like Admiral Swift and the pirates, this must be a ghostly apparition of the wolf's former self. But that didn't make it any less fearsome. Saliva dribbled from its

158

teeth and its blackened silhouette was the image of pure evil. It made a low rumbling sound.

This thing could swallow him whole if it wished.

'Stanley, what are you doing?' whimpered Daisy.

'Stay calm,' he answered. 'I don't know how on earth our werewolf got here, but I am sure that he comes to help us.'

The wolf eyed him closely, tilting its head at him. Stanley still had the stink of McCormick and Partridge about him and he could see that this troubled the spectre of the beast.

As the werewolf approached Stanley held his breath, slowly opening his coat so that the stench left by McCormick on his waistcoat was so strong it made him feel sick.

The beast sniffed at the foisty places where McCormick had been. A grumbling growl emanated from deep within, but still it did not move towards the pirates.

With growing confidence, Stanley set off towards Partridge and McCormick.

'I'm right with you, Stanley,' cried Daisy, trotting on behind. And through the corner of her eye, she could see the shape of the beast keeping close to them. It moved cat-like among the pines, slinking from tree trunk to tree trunk, weaving among the stones and boulders.

Stanley knew they didn't have much longer. They were nearing the evil pair, and he knew that if they saw them out here on the moor they would surely finish them both off.

Finally, the beast picked up the pirates'

scent from the ground and raced ahead of
Stanley and Daisy.

Stanley drew a shuddering sigh of relief,
as McCormick spotted the wolf and froze for
a second.

Partridge grasped at the rifle strapped to
his back. In a flash it was in his hands. He
blasted two shots at the wolf, but either they
missed or they simply made no difference.
The beast continued. Partridge reloaded and
fired again.

Stanley and Daisy were stuck in the field
of fire, crouching low behind rocks, dodging
the whistling bullets. But soon the wolf
was so close that the pirates' swords were
drawn. It was two on one … but surely
they wouldn't win against such a ferocious
beast.

McCormick and Partridge were swinging

their blades wildly while the monster tore at their arms and legs, lost in the swirling motion of battling man and beast.

Stanley wondered how he had ever overcome the beast. Partridge was wounded

again, and held his side as he forced himself
on. McCormick was down, and the beast
tossed him like a rag doll. Partridge took
another snap of the great powerful jaw – and
the pair was down and out.

Little by little, their spirits wisped up into the air, ghostly spinning shapes shooting like fireflies up into the black of midnight.

The wolf stood breathless, staring intently at Stanley, saliva still dropping from its open jaw. The snow and wind abruptly stopped and there was calm.

Wheezing badly, the beast dropped to the ground, its heart thumping in its chest.

Stanley ran forward.

'Careful, Stanley,' squeaked Daisy. 'Don't go too near!'

Nearby, the pike was lying forgotten in his case.

'Stanley, you are either brave or stupid. I am not sure which.'

But Stanley was unafraid. As he neared the wolf, he could see a large wound in its side. He fell to his knees in the freezing snow and softly stroked its weary head, its eyes half-open as if in sleep. Stanley wrapped his arms around the great body and tucked his frozen face into the warmth of its belly.

Running his hands through the wolf's long fur, Stanley felt its solid shape. With his head pressed to its chest, he listened to its beating heart slowing down. He held the wolf tight and watched as its spirit slowly died, the same flickering light soaring upward and disappearing.

'My father once said that even your greatest enemy is a friend somewhere along the road. You just need to take the trouble to make the journey and find out where,' sniffed Stanley.

Daisy took her hand out of her pocket and when she opened it, the tooth had disappeared.

Stanley felt a great sadness come over him. But as he glanced up, he realized that Partridge and McCormick had gone for ever. He and Daisy were safe, and the worst thing that could happen to them now was a roasting from Mrs Carelli.

'Perhaps you could come and get me now, if it isn't too much trouble,' grumbled the pike.

'I don't wish to lie in the snow all night. I
have had quite enough trial and tribulation
for one day.'

Daisy giggled. She had not heard the pike
speaking before.

The fish's huge mahogany case was
battered and broken and way too heavy
for Stanley to lift. As the storm died away,

the two friends removed the pike so that
Stanley could carry him neatly in his arms.
Then they headed home.

12

Not quite
the
End.

They had gone only a short way when
Stanley realized he was struggling with the
pike's weight.

'I'm sorry, I need to stop, Daisy.' He was
worn out and his arms had taken as much
punishment as they could manage.

'What a fuss about nothing,' teased Daisy.
She was always prepared for everything,

and produced a short length of rope from her coat pocket. Swiftly, she secured the pike on to Stanley's back.

'That's much better,' he declared, and they pushed on.

They decided to take a different route home; they'd gone so far across the moor that it would be easier to go back down past the lake, by the water mill and through the churchyard.

It was a relief not to feel the howling wind and snow battering at their faces. So much so that, what with getting rid of Partridge and McCormick as well, the journey home was almost pleasant. Bright moonlight lit their way and the worst thing they had to deal with was the heaving snow-drifts that crossed their path.

As they walked they chatted happily.

Stanley was looking forward to the next day, planning it in his head. They would sit around a great fire, drinking warm drinks and toasting marshmallows over the flames, and they wouldn't have a care in the world.

He smiled a big smile and looked across at Daisy. Soon his winter visit would be over, but for now he would make the best of the peace at Crampton Rock and his new-found friend.

They were nearing the lake now.

'Ah, the water. I can almost feel the ripples against my scales.'

It was the pike. He was awake again, mumbling to himself.

'I can smell it,' he continued. 'It is almost too hard to resist. Once, I was king there. I held council with many friends. I was held in high esteem … and now I sit wearily in my glass case, bearing despicable insults and harbouring stolen goods.'

His voice was growing louder.

'Please just go back to sleep, will you?' said Stanley. 'There's not far to go.'

The lake was in front of them now and as they passed by they saw that the surface was frozen. Stanley couldn't resist pressing his foot on to the ice, testing it until it made a cracking sound and a small fracture appeared.

'A *sardine!*' the pike cried. 'A sardine! How could she call *me* a sardine? I come from a long line of great and powerful pikes. I have the strength of a *million* sardines. My markings are distinguished and inimitable. How could she think I was anything else?'

'Please!' continued Stanley. 'I'm sure Mrs Carelli didn't wish to hurt you.'

Daisy concealed her amusement. 'Poor old Mister Pike,' she whispered. 'He has had a hard time lately. Perhaps he will settle once he is back in place and things are quieter. Now come on, Stanley. There's a warm fire waiting at home.'

This thought spurred Stanley into action. He turned sharply, ready to race after Daisy, but at that crucial moment his foot slipped. The pike jerked out of its bindings on his back and fell, sliding for a long moment before its weight pierced through the ice.

In what seemed like an instant it was gone, once more gliding through the shimmering water.

Stanley turned in horror. But it was too late – there was nothing he could do.

In some ways it was the best thing for the dear old fish. Indeed, it would not have mattered … but the Ibis was still lying in the stomach of the pike.

For the first time in a hundred years, every fragment of the Ibis's beautiful, delicate shape was surrounded by water. A ripple of tremors resounded across the earth and at that very moment, right there and then, the quickening began.

An ancient, crusty old treasure chest filled with aching bones lifted open ten thousand leagues under the sea, and a horde of fiendish skeletal forms began to assemble.

The soil moved beneath a gravestone out upon the moors of old England, to reveal a long purple-fingered hand searching through the dirt.

A tombstone was heaved to one side in Peru as two glimmering eyes stared out from the blackness.

From every darkened corner of the earth they began to move and soon, in all their ghastly forms, they would be on Crampton Rock.

Scribbles from the

Something Wickedly Weird

sketchbook.

Chris Mould

Chris Mould went to art school at the age of sixteen. During this time, he did various jobs, from delivering papers to washing-up and cooking in a kitchen. He has won the Nottingham Children's Book Award and been commended for the Sheffield. He loves his work and likes to write and draw the kind of books that he would have liked to have on his shelf as a boy. He is married with two children and lives in Yorkshire.

Crampton Rock seems the perfect place to spend a long summer holiday. But there's always something to go and spoil it all, isn't there?

Why are all the **dogs three-legged?**
Is there really a **werewolf** on the loose?
And what do the *pirates* want with Stanley Buggles...?

SOMETHING WICKEDLY WEIRD

The Werewolf and the Ibis

CHRIS MOULD

Up ahead, the shape of
Crampton Rock grows clear
through the misty glass of a hundred
telescopes. The black pirate swarm
moves ever closer for the final battle.

What has awoken the **skeletons** from their slumber?
And how can Stanley Buggles *escape*
from their deadly grip ...?

SOMETHING
WICKEDLY
WEIRD
The Buccaneer's Bones

CHRIS MOULD

The island of **Crampton Rock** has emerged from **pirate battle**. But something far more sinister is on the move...

What claim does the **Darkling family** have on Stanley Buggles' home?

And do the Darkling twins really keep a **two-headed snake** as a pet?

SOMETHING WICKEDLY WEIRD

The Curse of the Wolf

CHRIS MOULD

Stanley Buggles holds **the key** to the **smugglers' map**. But does he **dare** to uncover its **ancient secrets**?

What will happen if he ventures down into the **treacherous tunnels?**

And who is *following* behind . . .?

SOMETHING WICKEDLY WEIRD

The Smugglers' Secret

CHRIS MOULD

Are you prepared to be scared?

This book contains ten of the most terrifying tales, adapted, written and superbly illustrated by award-winner

Chris Mould.

Five are original ghost stories, and five are retellings of classic tales, from *The Legend of Sleepy Hollow* by Washington Irving to *The Tell-Tale Heart* by Edgar Allen Poe.

Open this book at your own peril ...